HELLO! WELCOME TO THE FABUMOUSE WORLD OF THE THEA SISTERS!

Thea Sisters

Hi, I'm Thea Stilton, Geronimo Stilton's sister! I am a special reporter for _The Rodent's Gazette_, the most famous newspaper on Mouse Island. I love traveling and meeting new mice all over the world, like the Thea Sisters. These five friends have helped me out with my adventures. Let me introduce you to these fabumouse young mice!

Colette has a real passion for fashion. She loves to design her own clothes in her favorite color, pink.

Violet loves studying and learning new things. She is a fan of classical music and dreams of becoming a famous violinist someday.

Pamela loves pizza so much she eats it for breakfast. She is a skilled mechanic who can fix just about any motor she gets her paws on.

PAULINA is shy and loves to read about faraway places. But she loves traveling to those places even more.

Nicky is from the Australian Outback, where she developed a love of nature and the environment. This outdoors-loving mouse is always on the move.

Thea Sisters

Thea Stilton

MOUSEFORD ACADEMY

DANCE
CHALLENGE

Scholastic Inc.

ISBN 978-0-545-67010-4

Copyright © 2010 by Edizioni Piemme S.p.A., Corso Como 15, 20154 Milan, Italy.

International Rights © Atlantyca S.p.A.

English translation © 2014 by Atlantyca S.p.A.

Based on an original idea by Elisabetta Dami.

www.geronimostilton.com

Published by Scholastic Inc., 557 Broadway, New York, NY 10012.
SCHOLASTIC and associated logos are trademarks and/or registered trademarks of Scholastic Inc.

Stilton is the name of a famous English cheese. It is a registered trademark of the Stilton Cheese Makers' Association. For more information, go to www.stiltoncheese.com.

Text by Thea Stilton
Original title *Sfida a ritmo di danza!*
Cover by Giuseppe Facciotto
Illustrations by Francesco Castelli
Graphics by Yuko Egusa

Special thanks to Beth Dunfey
Translated by Emily Clement
Interior design by Becky James

12 11 10 9 8 7 6 5 4 3   15 16 17 18 19/0

Printed in the U.S.A.   40
First printing, September 2014

WELCOME BACK, MOUSELETS!

A cool BREEZE blew through the port at Whale Island, carrying the crisp scent of autumn along with it.

Mouseford Academy was just opening after the long SUMMER break, and Vince Guymouse's ferryboat was filled with chattering students. They were thrilled to be back with their friends again.

"**Come on, mouselings!**" called Pamela, scampering off the ship with Colette, Nicky, Paulina, and Violet. "I have a feeling lots of fabumouse surprises are waiting for us this year."

"You said it!" Nicky said. "I can't wait to check out the creative writing class."

"And I'm looking forward to my violin lessons," said Violet, *smiling*.

"Mouselets, aren't you forgetting the most important thing?" Colette interrupted.

"Of course!" Pamela remembered. "The headmaster promised us that we'd have *acting*, *singing*, and *dancing* lessons this year."

With a squeak of glee, Paulina grabbed Pamela by the paw. Together the two rodents glided into a graceful tango.

"**HOLEY CHEESE**, you're way ahead of the rest of us!" Colette laughed. "A special class dedicated to music and theater sounds so fun."

"Yes, it will be absolutely *fabumouse*," Nicky agreed. "Let's all sign up!"

"*Friends together, mice forever!*" the mouselets cheered.

Hooray!

Yay!

The Thea Sisters' enthusiasm attracted the attention of their classmates Tanja and Craig, who were also **scrambling** off the ferry.

"Howdy, mouselets!" Craig greeted them. "So good to see you! What are you five *celebrating*?"

"We can't wait to start that new drama class," Paulina explained.

"This year, we'll have something to **sing** about," warbled Nicky, pretending there was a microphone in her paw.

"**HA, HA, HA!**" Tanja laughed. "So you're planning to sign up, too? I've been

4

dreaming about it all summer."

Shen scurried over to the little group.

"I've been preparing for drama class, too," he said, pointing to the SUITCASE he was  dragging behind him. "I've got all the most important plays from the last hundred years in there. I want to make a good impression on the new professor!"

"Well, I'm not sure the theater is the best showcase for talent as big as mine," joked Craig, sticking his snout in the air snobbishly. Then he grabbed Violet by the paw and sent her into a series of twirls that made her tail spin!

His friends burst into applause, encouraging the dancers. With every twist

and turn, they drew closer to Shen's suitcase. Closer and closer, until . . .

KABLAM!

The two rodents bumped right into the suitcase, knocking it over with a spectacular **CRASH**!

Nicky leaned over and gave Craig and Violet a helping paw. "For now, maybe we should just try to get to class in **one** piece!" she said, laughing.

THE NEW
PROFESSOR

Violet and Craig had just gotten back on their paws when Elly Squid scurried up to them. "Come on, rodents, shake a tail! The headmaster is heading this way to greet the new teacher."

"I can't wait to meet her!" Pam exclaimed. "Professor Ratyshnikov is a real CELEBRITY!" She and her friends headed toward the small STAGE that the headmaster had set up to welcome the new professor.

"She's directed more than thirty plays and musicals. She's a true LEGEND," Paulina agreed.

"I heard she brought her best assistants

to teach us," Tanja put in.

"Moldy mozzarella! I absolutely must find something to wear for the first class," Colette murmured.

"If I were you, I'd think twice before changing my whole WARDROBE, Colette," a voice squeaked sharply. "A class this exclusive certainly isn't for everyone!"

The mouselets turned. There was only one rodent who would make that kind of comment: **Ruby Flashyfur**!

The mouselet was sashaying toward them, surrounded by her faithful friends, the Ruby Crew. She looked over each of the Thea Sisters from snout to paw before continuing.

"Of course, you could always

try out, if you have the **nerve** . . ."

"Of course we have the nerve!" Pamela spluttered indignantly.

"We'll practice and work hard, just like we always do," Nicky added **proudly**. But Ruby and her friends just flounced away with their snouts in the air.

Throughout this whole exchange, Violet was as **quiet** as a mouse. She was thinking hard. Her father was an orchestra conductor, and her mother was a singer. She'd heard them squeaking about Professor Ratyshnikov.

Mouseford's newest instructor had been a famous ballerina, and she was known all over the world as a great artist . . . with a **terrible** personality! She had a reputation for being demanding and strict — and for squeaking sharply to her students and assistants.

Violet **SUSPECTED** that Professor Ratyshnikov's class would be difficult in more ways than one, but she didn't want to **alarm** her friends until she met the teacher for herself. So she said nothing.

"**Come on**, let's go," Elly exclaimed. "Professor Ratyshnikov's motorboat is about to arrive!"

A STRANGE
WELCOME

Sure enough, a large white motorboat was rumbling into the harbor.

All the students were buzzing. They milled around the dock, stretching to get a look at the **FAMOUSE** director. The entire faculty had crowded nearby.

Octavius de Mousus, Mouseford Academy's headmaster, seemed agitated. He couldn't stop pacing BACK and FORTH like a cat outside a mousehole.

"Is my tie on straight?" he asked Professor Marblemouse, tugging on his shirt collar. "The stage is **big** enough, right?" he asked Professor Sparkle, who reassured him for the hundredth time.

Then the headmaster dug into his pockets. "And my speech? Where did I put my speech?" he cried. Professor Rattcliff pawed him a few **sheets** of paper, shaking her snout patiently.

"Even the headmaster seems **nervous**," Paulina whispered to her friends.

"Yeah," Colette agreed. "This new class must be really **important**!"

Um...am I ready?

Finally, the motorboat docked. A moment later, a **slender**, *elegant* rodent with long blond fur appeared on the gangplank.

As soon as the rodent's paws touched solid ground, the headmaster began his speech. He was stuttering with *excitement*.

"Friends, students, colleagues, I am proud

to present to you Professor Ratyshnikov, the leader of our new department of Arts, Music, and Theater," he squeaked proudly. "This is a **NEW** chapter in the prestigious history of Mouseford Academy!"

The students and teachers all applauded. But Professor Ratyshnikov didn't even crack a smile. She stepped forward with an air of **indifference**.

Professor Datamouse gave the headmaster an ornately carved **BOX**. Professor de Mousus took it with both paws and extended it toward the new instructor.

But Professor Ratyshnikov turned her snout away. "Thank you for everything, Octavius, but I absolutely detest these ceremonies! You should have known better."

The headmaster grew as still as a **BLOCK** of aged cheddar. Before he

could squeak, the new professor added, "We have a lot of work to do. There's no reason to waste any more time hanging around here!"

With that, she strode away, heading for the academy. After a few **awkward** moments, everyone followed her.

An Intriguing
Mystery

"That was weird!" Paulina squeaked as she headed toward campus with the other Thea Sisters. They were all surprised by the **SHARP** tone the new professor had used with the headmaster.

"I wonder what was inside that beautiful box," Nicky reflected.

"Hmm . . ." Pamela wondered. "Yeah, me, too."

"I'll bet it was a *special* welcome gift," Violet put in.

Just then, a flaming **RED** convertible stopped next to them.

It was Professor Bartholomew Sparkle.

Pamela seized the chance to ask him

about the ceremony. "That was **strange**, don't you think, Professor?" She was hoping he could tell them a little more about the **mysterious** Professor Ratyshnikov.

Professor Sparkle nodded. "Of course, none of the staff expected the ceremony to be cut short like that," he agreed. "Though the headmaster did warn us that Professor Ratyshnikov can be more PRICKLY than a porcupine!"

So they already know each other?

"So the headmaster already knows Professor Ratyshnikov?" Violet asked.

"That's right," the professor said. "I've heard he and Professor Ratyshnikov were fast **FRIENDS** back when they attended Mouseford together. But then something happened, and she left the academy very suddenly, without graduating."

"Do you mean Professor Ratyshnikov 𝖖𝖚𝖎𝖙?!" Colette asked in surprise.

"That's what they say, but unfortunately that's all I know about it," Professor Sparkle said. "Well, I must be off! I'll see you in class, mouselets." He drove away.

"So the headmaster and Professor Ratyshnikov have known each other since they were very young, but then something happened to **SEPARATE** them," Pamela said slowly.

"Uh-huh," Nicky confirmed. "Don't you want to find out what? *I'm more curious than a cat!*"

PROPS IN THEIR PROPER PLACE

When the Thea Sisters reached the academy, a large red truck was **BLOCKING** the main entrance. A crowd of students had gathered, and they were unloading strangely shaped objects. Tanja, Craig, and Shen were among them. Their paws were full of colorful boxes and packages.

"Mouselets, give us a paw!" Tanja called out. "We have to carry these COSTUMES, WIGS, and PROPS inside."

"Yeah, we need all the help we can get," said Craig, who was bent under the weight of a large mirror. "It looks like we're going to BUILD a whole new theater!"

As the students struggled with their loads,

Give us a paw!

a rodent with a cheerful snout popped out of the truck.

Paulina nudged Colette. "Hey, I think that's the new drama teacher, **PROFESSOR ROBERT PLOTFUR**!"

The professor sprang out of the truck.

"Come on, move those paws, mouselings!"

he cried, brushing a lock of fur off his forehead.

A few moments later, another new teacher stopped by. It was Professor Rosalyn Plié, the dance professor.

PROFESSOR ROBERT PLOTFUR

Professor Plotfur hadn't noticed her yet —

he was busy unloading his **TRUCK**. The young professor glided toward him gracefully. "Hi, Professor Plotfur. Good to see you again."

"Hey there, Professor Plié!" he replied, giving her a **BOX** full of costumes and wigs. "You've arrived just in the nick of time."

"Um . . . what's this?" Professor Plié stuttered, staggering under the box's weight.

Professor Rosalyn Plié

"Lend me a paw, please, I have to **hurry**!" Professor Plotfur said as he scurried inside the building. "I just remembered I left the **FAUCET** running in my room. I don't want to

flood the academy on my first day!"

"That's Professor Plotfur for you . . . always with his snout in the stratosphere!"

said Professor Plié. She rolled her eyes affectionately.

LIKE A
THUNDERBOLT!

The Thea Sisters immediately offered Professor Plié their help.

"I'm PAMELA, and this is **Violet**, *Nicky*, PAULINA, and *Colette*," Pamela said, taking a box of wigs out of the new professor's paws.

"Thank you very much, mouselets," the instructor said warmly. "We still need to get settled, but it's a great pleasure to be teaching at this academy."

"You're part of the new THEATER department, right?" Violet asked, lifting another **BOX**.

"Exactly!" Professor Plié answered. She and the Thea Sisters had entered the academy and were heading toward the drama classroom. "Our department was created by Professor Ratyshnikov. She's divided the ᴄʟᴀss into three **sections**: one in acting, taught by Professor Plotfur; one in dance, which is mine; and then there's ᴘʀᴏꜰᴇssᴏʀ ᴀɴɴᴀ ᴀʀɪᴀ, your singing teacher." Professor Plié pointed to Professor Ratyshnikov's third instructor.

A lively young rodent whose fur was streaked with ᴄᴏʟᴏʀꜰᴜʟ strands stood at the door to the classroom. But before the Thea Sisters could introduce themselves, loud music started **thumping**.

The singing teacher was instantly surrounded by a ɴᴏɪsʏ throng of students,

ᴘʀᴏꜰᴇssᴏʀ ᴀɴɴᴀ ᴀʀɪᴀ

pushing their way into the classroom to see what was **happening**. The Thea Sisters and Professor Plié couldn't help but join them.

Ruby and her crew had been practicing all morning. They were determined to **impress** their new teachers, and they had decided to perform right there, in front of everyone.

We're the Ruby Crew!

"TWO, THREE, FOUR!"

shouted Ruby.

In the blink of a cat's eye, Zoe, Alicia, and Connie stepped into formation and began performing a song and dance number.

"I can't believe it!" exclaimed Pamela, shocked. "This time Ruby has really outdone herself!"

"Um, are those mouselets your **friends**?" Professor Plié whispered.

"Not exactly," Paulina replied.

"Well, they certainly had an ORIGINAL idea," the professor commented. "But I know each student at this school has a SPECIAL talent inside."

Professor Plié smiled at them.

"In my class, you'll learn to show your inner *grace* and agility. And Professor Ratyshnikov will teach you how best to

use your **STRENGTH** and energy!
These qualities are all very important in
dance. Soon you'll all know how to express
yourselves through movement."

The Thea Sisters exchanged eager looks.
The new class sounded really exciting!

Meanwhile, Ruby and her friends were
still dancing and singing. Then suddenly a
firm, strict squeak interrupted them.

"Who is responsible for that awful shrieking?!"

Professor Ratyshnikov swept into the
classroom, with the headmaster trailing
behind her.

Ruby stopped singing and dancing
instantly, as did Alicia and Zoe. Connie was
so embarrassed, she hid her snout in her
PAWS.

Zoe hurried to turn off the music. Her fur had turned **redder** than a Gouda cheese rind.

An awkward silence fell over the room. All the students were intimidated. Professor Ratyshnikov looked *stricter* than a barn owl on a rodent-free diet.

The professor stared at the Ruby Crew. Then her eyes swept over the rest of the **STUDENTS**. "Well, since there are so many students here, why don't I take this opportunity to look you over?" she said. "Let's see what we've got!"

Who's shrieking?!

Oops!

A STORM BREWING

Professor Ratyshnikov turned away from the Ruby Crew and toward Colette, Nicky, Pam, Paulina, and Violet!

"Ah yes, let me introduce some of our *finest* students, the Thea Sisters," the headmaster squeaked. He gestured toward Colette, who bowed nervously.

Passable, but barely . . .

"Yes, very nice," said the professor, *examining* Colette with a **critical** eye. "You are rather graceful . . . but you don't seem to

Straighten your back!

know what to do with your 🐾🐾🐾🐾!"

Then she moved on to Violet, who curtseyed. "You have the body of a dancer, young mouselet. But what's going on with that arched back?"

Professor Ratyshnikov turned to Paulina, who was twisting her long braid. "You look agile enough, but you must stop fidgeting! And you," she said, turning to Pamela. "Good muscles,

Don't fidget!

Too stiff!

but your posture is **STIFFER** than a moldy cheese stick!"

Nicky took a step forward, thinking she might as well get it over with. Professor Ratyshnikov looked her over from **snout** to **toe**.

"You have good paws, but be careful with them, we're not on a **SOCCER** field!"

Ruby Flashyfur was enjoying the Thea Sisters' stunned expressions.

Finally, Ruby thought.

Watch your paws.

Someone figured out how to wipe the **smug** *smiles off those mouselets' snouts!*

"I've seen enough," Professor Ratyshnikov continued. "I strongly recommend that you all enroll in my class if you want to acquire any *elegance* and *grace*."

The headmaster cleared his throat. "Students, you are in for a unique **experience**! Professor Ratyshnikov and her class represent something entirely **NEW** for this institution, and I'm sure you'll all seize this marvemouse op —"

"Yes, you all simply must sign up," Professor Ratyshnikov interrupted. "For years, my students have gone on to become world-class performers. It's about time **MOUSEFORD ACADEMY** recognized my talent!"

The **headmaster** drew Professor Ratyshnikov aside. "My dear professor, I can assure you that these students are among your greatest admirers," he whispered. "They're eager to study under your brilliant tutelage."

Professor Ratyshnikov was unmoved. "Are you sure that things have changed so much since —" She stopped abruptly, leaving the words hanging in EMPTY air. Then she called to her assistant professors and scurried away.

The Thea Sisters had been standing close enough to overhear this heated exchange between the headmaster and Professor Ratyshnikov. Colette raised her eyebrows CURIOUSLY.

On the other paw, Ruby and her friends hadn't noticed the conversation between the two professors. They were too busy giggling over what the new professor had said to the

Thea Sisters.

Ruby was enchanted by the new instructor's personality. Professor Ratyshnikov was famouse, fascinating, *elegant*, and above all,

This could be my big break!

she struck fear into the fur of the rodents around her. These were exactly the qualities Ruby herself **hoped** to develop!

"Zoe! Alicia! Connie!" Ruby called to her friends. "We **absolutely** must sign up for that class. This could be my big break, and I'm not letting anything or **anyone** stop me!"

A PEEK INTO
THE PAST

The Thea Sisters gathered around as Ruby, Connie, Zoe, and Alicia scampered off to their **rooms**.

"This new class seems like it's going to be tougher than a temperamental tomcat," Pamela said. "But I love a challenge, don't you? **We'll just have to give it our all!**"

"Don't forget, we also have to uncover the truth about the headmaster and Professor Ratyshnikov's **past**," Violet said. "Every time he tries to do something nice for her . . ."

"She gets more **FURIOUS** than a fly in fondue!" Paulina concluded.

"It's true," Colette mused. "Hey, did anyone else notice her gorgeous fur? I wonder if she uses the same CUCUMBER OIL as me."

"Yet another big mystery to solve," replied Pamela, giggling.

"Hey, Professor Ratyshnikov was a student at the academy, right?" said Paulina. "Maybe we could find CLUES about her history in the Hall of Records."

"**Great idea**," Pamela replied. "The Hall of Records has a **photo** of every student who ever came to the academy."

The mouselets scurried through the herb garden and entered the North Tower, which led them directly to the Hall of Records.

"**LOOK!**" Nicky exclaimed, pointing to a photo on the wall. "Remember? That's from our first year at the academy!"

"Do you remember how new and **EXCITING** it all was back then?" Paulina sighed.

"Yeah!" Nicky said. "And look, there's **THEA**."

Colette smiled. "Just think about how many roads she's traveled since then."

"And how many we have, too!" Pamela added with a grin.

Violet was scanning the walls for a **photo** of Professor Ratyshnikov.

THEA
STILTON

"To find her, we'll need to go back to photos from many years ago — wait, here we go. **THESE ARE THE PICTURES WE'RE LOOKING FOR!**"

BOOMER'S TALE

Just then, a familiar squeak distracted the Thea Sisters. "Are you **LOOKING** for something, mouselets?"

It was Boomer Whale, the academy's handymouse. Boomer knew every detail of Mouseford's history, and he took his job seriously. Every day, he **dusted** the photographs from one end of the hall to the other.

"Hi, Boomer," Nicky said. "We're looking for a photo of Professor Ratyshnikov. We heard she attended the academy back when she was a mouselet."

"That's right," Boomer replied. "I was just a **mouselet** myself back then, but I used to help my father when he had this job. I remember Miss Ratyshnikov very well. She was a **lively** mouselet who was full of ideas — a bit like the five of you! In fact, she was the one who founded the **Lizard Club**!"

"Wait, Professor Ratyshnikov created our club?" Pamela asked, dumbfounded.

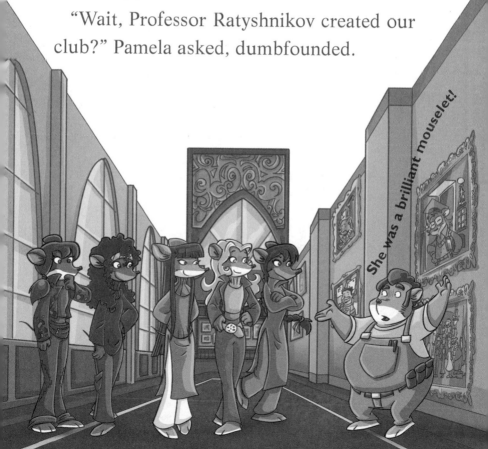

She was a brilliant mouselet!

"That's right," Boomer said. "It was a completely **NEW** and groundbreaking idea. Up until then, the academy had the Gecko Club, which was only for male mice. Miss Ratyshnikov fought for **EQUALITY** between males and females here at Mouseford. Unfortunately, she was up against a very **STRICT**, old-fashioned headmaster!"

Boomer pointed to a photograph of a stern-looking rodent with long, white **WHISKERS**. "He gave Miss Ratyshnikov

a challenge: 'If you want a club of your own, you must win a competition against the mice in the Gecko Club,'" Boomer continued.

Violet listened with bated breath. "So what

did Professor Ratyshnikov do?"

"She accepted the challenge, of course!" Boomer said. "But **something** went wrong during the competition, and she ended up leaving the academy. I never knew what happened, but it must've been something **terrible**, because Miss Ratyshnikov never came back. It was tragic, really, because she got her wish — the mouselets' club was founded, but by then it was too late for her to **enjoy** it."

The Thea Sisters thanked the handymouse and headed toward their dorm.

"So what do you think happened?" Violet asked.

"I don't know," said Colette. "I'm more **confused** than ever!"

"Me, too," said Nicky. "And I wonder how the headmaster was **involved**...."

A NEW CHALLENGE

The next morning, Pamela scampered through the academy's halls, shouting, "Move those tails, mouselets, or we'll be late for sign-up!"

They were just a few moments away from

Come on!

the first **session** of the new **class**. Right now the **challenge** between the Geckos and the Lizards seemed like ancient history!

The headmaster had reserved the **GYMNASIUM** for Professor Ratyshnikov's first class.

Light was shining through

the large windows, reflecting off the enormouse **MIRRORS**. Ballet **barres** lined the walls. Chairs had been lined up for the students hoping to earn a place in the class.

Professor Ratyshnikov and her three **assistant professors** were already in the gym. The mouselets took their seats silently, intimidated by the stern look on the professor's snout. Luckily, Professor Plié greeted the Thea Sisters with a big **smile**.

Ruby was the last student to enter the classroom. She crossed the room with her snout held high. Her friends had saved her a seat in the front **ROW**.

Nicky noticed that Ryder Flashyfur was there, too, at the very back of the room. Ruby's **brother** liked to play it cooler than cottage cheese, but it seemed the new

class had aroused his curiosity, too.

As soon as everyone was seated, Professor Ratyshnikov began **squeaking**. "Mouseford students, I am pleased to offer you this class on the dramatic arts. It will be taught at the highest level, which is why you'll need to audition in order to enroll."

At the word **AUDITION**, an anxious ripple passed through the students. But Professor Ratyshnikov stopped the murmurs with an **icy** look.

"To earn a spot in my class, you must demonstrate that you know how to **dance**, that you understand **music**, that you can sing in tune, and that you have the gift of interpretation," she went on. "And let me make one final thing clear: I will not tolerate cheating of any kind!"

"We'll do our best!" Paulina squeaked

before she could stop herself. Professor Ratyshnikov's words had rubbed her fur the wrong way. "If there's one thing we've learned here at the academy, it's how to work **honestly** and diligently."

"We'll see about that," the professor sniffed. "Those who wish to try their luck will have one week to prepare a dance audition with COSTUMES, **music**, and LIGHTS!"

We always work our hardest!

With that, Professor Ratyshnikov swept from the classroom, leaving the students CHATTERING nervously in her wake.

"Did you hear that, mouselets?" Violet cried. "Is it me, or does Professor

Ratyshnikov seem to have a **grudge** against the whole academy?"

Colette nodded. "It's almost as if she's expecting us to fail."

Pam was frowning. "And she seems to think we'll try to cheat!"

"**Snouts up, sisters!**" Nicky exclaimed. "We'll convince Professor Ratyshnikov that she's **WRONG** by earning spots at the top of her class!"

DON'T BE SCARED OFF!

Professor Ratyshnikov's three assistant professors stayed in the gymnasium to squeak with the students.

"The auditions will be challenging, but don't let that scare you off," Professor Aria began.

"We're asking you to do a lot of work," continued Professor Plotfur, "but we're not expecting perfection."

Professor Plié nodded. "The theme of the show will be the WORLD THROUGH DANCE! Each team must use dance to express the way they see the world around them."

"What a cool challenge!" Nicky said.

"It could be really FUN," Violet agreed.

"We're going to split you into small groups, but first we need to get to know you better," Professor Aria explained. "We'd like to see you one at a time so we can figure out which group you'd fit into best."

"We'll call you in alphabetical order," added Professor Plotfur, trying to read the **MESSY** sign-up list. "Or maybe we'll just go in random order!" He put the **SHEET** back on the desk.

The students filed into the **hallway** to wait their turns.

"I have no idea what's waiting for us in there," Paulina whispered to Violet.

Her friend took her paw. "Don't worry! When you're in there, it'll just be you, and you'll be **great**!"

One by one, the students were called into the gymnasium, each with his or her tail in a twist. But by the time they finished, they seemed LIGHT as freshly grated Parmesan. The rodents started chatting with one another about their assignment.

At the end of the day, the students returned to the gym to be divided up. The Thea Sisters were all assigned to the same dance group. Their team included Elly and Tanja for costume design and Shen for music and lights. The band of friends celebrated the good news with a round of **hugs** and high-fives.

Ruby was in good spirits, too. She'd been assigned to a team with the Ruby Crew, and they were working with Ryder, Sebastian, and Craig.

A spiteful look crept across her snout as she glanced over at the Thea Sisters. "**YOU'D BETTER CELEBRATE WHILE YOU CAN, MY**

DEAR MOUSELINGS," she murmured under her breath. "Because we're going to make Swiss cheese out of you!"

SHINING LIGHT ON THE PAST

As the Thea Sisters were heading out of the **GYM**, Professor Plié approached Paulina.

"You know, Paulina, I really **appreciated** what you said during the professor's speech," she said. "**Honesty** and hard work are important, and I'm sure that you'll all do your best."

The other mouselets were curious, so Paulina took the opportunity to ask a question. "Why is Professor Ratyshnikov so **HARD** on the headmaster and the academy?"

Professor Plié sighed. "Professor Ratyshnikov is a very **challenging** teacher. Ever since she left Mouseford, she has demanded as much of her students as she does of hER$ELF."

"We know she had to compete against the GECKO CLUB," Paulina said, "but what happened after that? Why did she leave the **ACADEMY**?"

It's a story from years ago . . . .

"I'm afraid I don't have all the details," Professor Plié began. "But I do know that the current **HEADMASTER**, Octavius de Mousus, was the president of the Gecko Club at the time of the challenge. Professor Ratyshnikov had to face him in a series of **competitions**, even though they were good friends at the time."

It was so quiet, you could hear a cheese slice drop. The **mouselets** were hanging on to every word of the professor's story.

"After the first challenge, the two teams were tied. Then, during the math challenge,

RUNNING RACE

Professor Ratyshnikov pushed the mouselets' team into the lead. But it wasn't over: The final test was an **athletic** contest. Professor Ratyshnikov's team was super prepared, but something went **wrong**, and the Geckos won.

"Professor Ratyshnikov accused Professor de Mousus's team of **cheating**. But the

headmaster at that time wouldn't hear a word of it. So she decided to quit."

"What a sad story," said Colette. "That's a terrible way for a friendship to end!"

Paulina looked worried. "I just can't believe Professor de Mousus would sabotage Professor Ratyshnikov's team," she said. "That doesn't seem like him."

"You're right, Paulina," Violet said. "He's always taught us to behave honestly and HONORABLY."

"Sisters, something stinks worse than rotten Gouda," said Pam. "Looks like we've got a job to do."

Nicky nodded. "We've got to show Professor Ratyshnikov the academy is a fair place now," Nicky said. "And help the headmaster repair an old friendship!"

BEWARE OF SPIES

The next day, the Thea Sisters' team met to prepare for their performance.

Colette had the perfect song for their audition. She brought a **STEREO** to play it for her friends. The melody began with a **sweet**, sad theme that gradually became *LIVELY*, until it exploded into a rhythm bursting with energy!

"You like it, right?" Colette said happily. Her friends were shaking their snouts and tapping their tails to the **rhythm**. "I've loved this piece since I was little. Don't you think it would work for our audition?"

"It's beautiful, Colette!" Paulina exclaimed.

"If we rearrange it here and there, we could make it a bit more **modern**," Nicky suggested.

"And with lights, we can create just the right atmosphere!" Shen added.

Tanja thought about the COSTUMES. "What do you say to colors inspired by SUMMERTIME?"

"Yes, bright, warm colors . . . that sounds perfect!" Elly added.

Violet stood up. "Great! How about a nice cup of **tea** to get us started?"

"Don't forget the **cheese slices**!" said Pam. She was always hungry. "A whole heap of 'em!"

Little did the mouselets realize that someone was **lurking** in the hallway outside their classroom. She was carrying a

duster and wore a large apron and a green kerchief over her fur. It was Zoe!

You see, the Ruby Crew was determined to do whatever it took to **WIN**. Ruby was making a **MYSTERIOUS** telephone call, and Alicia and Connie were scouring all the costume stores on the island. But Zoe had the most important job: spying on the Thea Sisters!

Zoe crept closer and closer to the door of the room where the mousclets' group was meeting. She listened carefully, trying to memorize every note of the melody.

But when Violet scampered out of the classroom to make the tea . . .

The door swung open and smacked Zoe right in the snout!

"Yee-ouch!" she cried. She quickly jumped to her  and scurried away. The last thing Zoe wanted was to blow her cover. She had run a big **risk**, but she'd accomplished her mission!

¡ SMELL A RAT!

While the Ruby Crew was plotting, the Thea Sisters' group was preparing for the AUDITION.

Over the next few days, the teams took turns rehearsing in the large, MIRRORED classroom that Professor Ratyshnikov had reserved for her class.

"*Come on, mouselets!*" Paulina called to her friends as they all headed to practice. "It's our turn!"

"Shhh!" Violet suddenly whispered. "Listen! Doesn't that TUNE sound familiar?!"

"Slimy Swiss balls!" cried Nicky. "Someone's been spying on us!"

The mouselets burst into the classroom, where a **TERRIBLE** surprise awaited them: The Ruby Crew was practicing to the notes of their music!

Pam was **boiling** like a pot of forgotten fondue. "Where did you get this music?!"

"Do you like it?" Ruby asked innocently. "We chose it for our audition, and Professor Ratyshnikov L-O-V-E-D it. She told us we'd made a fabumouse selection!"

Zoe, Connie, and Alicia exchanged a **nasty** look as they stifled their giggles.

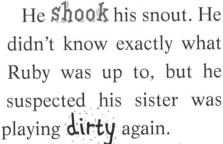

In the far corner of the room, Ryder stopped practicing.

He **shook** his snout. He didn't know exactly what Ruby was up to, but he suspected his sister was playing **dirty** again.

Colette had tears of disappointment in her eyes. "You can't do that! This music is ours!"

"Don't worry, Colette," said Pamela, leading her friend away by the paw. "We'll find another piece of music that's even better. You'll see!"

"Pam's right," Nicky agreed. "It's the only thing we can do. We have no way to prove that low-down, sneaky mouselet stole our music!"

"But how did they find out about our song?" Paulina asked in disbelief.

Violet instantly remembered the moment a few days earlier when someone had SLIPPED outside their rehearsal room door. "I smell a rat," she declared. "Someone was eavesdropping when we chose our MUSIC."

"You don't have a shred of **PROOF**!" Ruby cried.

"Come on, mouselets," said Shen. "It's not worth wasting any more **time** on these sneaks! Let's go make a **plan**."

There was nothing else for the Thea Sisters' team to do. So they went back to the Lizard Club's meeting room, dragging their tails behind them.

Hee, hee, hee!

HISTORY REPEATING ITSELF

Colette, Nicky, Pamela, Paulina, Violet, Tanja, Elly, and Shen scurried silently through the **hallways**. In a moment, all their work had disappeared like cheddar in a cheese grater, and now they only had **two**

days left to prepare for their audition!

"It'll be hard to find a piece of MUSIC that's just as beautiful for our audition," Tanja murmured sadly.

The students had reached the academy's main entrance. There they ran into another rodent roaming the hallways unhappily — the headmaster. He was in a BLACK mood, and his whiskers were droopy.

Professor de Mousus was heading in the OPPOSITE direction from the mouselets. He and Pamela almost bumped snouts.

"Oh, hello, students," the headmaster greeted them. "How are you?"

"Not great," Pamela grumbled. "We're having a hard time with our audition for the new class."

The headmaster sighed. "Every test presents its own challenges, but also its own opportunity to learn and grow."

"But Professor Ratyshnikov's assignment is so DIFFICULT!" Shen said.

"Yeah," continued Tanja. "It almost seems like she's making it impossible on purpose!"

"Don't think that Professor Ratyshnikov doesn't appreciate your efforts," the headmaster replied. "She has overcome huge obstacles of her own . . ."

"Do you mean the contest for the Lizard Club?" Paulina asked.

The headmaster twisted his whiskers. "Ah, so you've already heard about the challenge that led to her departure."

"But how did it happen?" Colette asked. "And why?"

The headmaster shook his snout sadly. "Unfortunately, Professor Ratyshnikov was right: Someone SABO⊗TAGED her team!"

She was right!

SABOTAGE!

"Unbelievable!" Colette said. "But who could have wanted to see Professor Ratyshnikov **FAIL**?"

The headmaster **sighed**. "Robert Shadysnout, who was a member of my **TEAM**!"

Shen and the mouselets held their breath, curious to hear the rest of the sad story.

"Robert was dead set against the idea of a club for female mice," the headmaster continued, "but I didn't think he would stoop to cheating! The night before the final challenge, he spread **OLIVE OIL** on all the athletic equipment, making it impossible to grab or catch anything. Needless to squeak, the mouselets' **ATHLETIC** exhibition was a cat-astrophe!"

"**What a cold-hearted cheat!**" Nicky cried.

The **headmaster** nodded. "He really pulled the cheesecloth over my eyes. Professor Ratyshnikov blamed my team, and she quit the academy. I began to believe her **SUSPICIONS**, so I tried to find the culprit."

"That's when you realized Robert Shadysnout had been up to **NO GOOD**?" Violet asked.

"Yes," the headmaster confirmed. "I found a **CANISTER** of oil in Shadysnout's bedroom closet, and he confessed."

"But Professor Ratyshnikov had already left, and you had lost touch," Paulina deduced.

"Exactly!" the headmaster sighed. "It was only years later that I tracked her down and told her what had happened. She was glad to know the truth, but her trust in me and in Mouseford was already destroyed. I doubt she'll ever forgive me!"

The mouselets and Shen WATCHED the headmaster walk away with the same

sad, preoccupied expression he'd had when they ran into him.

"**Crusty carburetors!**" Pamela cried. "We've got to do something to **help** him."

"That's a nice idea, Pam, but how?" Violet wondered. "We're already in big **trouble** with our audition."

Paulina sighed. "We're stuck like rats in a maze! We need time to think."

"What do you say to a **WALK** down to the docks?" Nicky suggested. "We could use some fresh air — and some fresh ideas!"

INSPIRATION AT THE DOCKS

The students stepped outside under the clear, blue sky. Nicky took a deep breath. Moments ago, she'd been moodier than a muskrat. But being outside always cheered her up. She was starting to feel better already.

A few minutes later, they'd reached the seaport. Now it was Pam's turn to breathe deeply. "Mmm . . . the smell of the sea."

"I just love these vibrant colors," Paulina commented, watching the waves reflect the golden beams of the sun.

"The sounds of the ocean always calm me down," said Violet. "Listen!"

The mice all stopped squeaking for a moment. The sounds of the sea and the

harbor filled the air around them:

FFRR . . . SSHH!
BONG! BONG!
CLOMP! CLANG!

The lapping of the waves, the faint clang of the lighthouse bells, even the clatter of metal containers opening and closing — all the sounds seemed connected, creating a steady rhythm.

"Listen to that beat!" said Pamela.

The mouselets all began to sway, tapping their paws to the rhythm.

"Flying fish sticks, I think we've got it!" Pam declared. "This is it, rodents! It's the perfect music for our audition."

"Yes!" Colette agreed excitedly. "For the

choreography, we could move like the ocean **waves** and the sea birds!"

"And our costumes could reflect the changing colors of the ocean," added Tanja.

"Mixed with the bright colors of the seaport," Elly continued.

"I'll take care of the music," Shen said. "I can definitely recreate the sounds of the seaport!"

"Hmm, I'd love to bring together **DIFFERENT** rhythms and styles in the choreography," Tanja reflected.

"Ballet!" Colette suggested.

"Hip-hop!" Pamela added.

"Gymnastics!" Nicky declared.

"Jazz!" Violet interjected.

"And don't forget the tango!" Paulina cried.

"It's really inspired!" Nicky exclaimed. Pam grinned. "I love it when a plan comes together!"

"This is totally us," Colette concluded, beaming. "And this is the world we want to express **through dance**!"

A MASKED BALL

Back on campus, the Ruby Crew was struggling with their rehearsals. They had the music they wanted, but the choreography was more of a challenge than anyone had expected.

"Move those paws!" Ruby shouted at her friends. "You're all hopeless."

The rodents were exhausted. Ruby had bought heavy, ELABORATE costumes that made every step difficult. The dancers' awkward movements looked ridiculous under all the folds of fabric.

"We're too tired to move," said Ryder.

"My paws hurt," Alicia moaned. "And Craig keeps stepping on my paws!"

Zoe slumped to the ground, gasping. "Just admit it, Ruby — our dance is a total disaster!"

Oops . . .

Ouch!

Ruby's eyes were shining. "I know it is." She smiled. "But don't tell me you seriously thought I'd let you cheesebrains make a FOOL out of me."

Connie stopped. "What are you saying?"

A TRIUMPHANT expression crossed Ruby's snout. "Well, in spite of your total lack of talent, our audition is guaranteed to be a smashing success!"

The rodents gathered around Ruby as she revealed her SECRET plan.

"As soon as I heard about the audition, I called my mom and asked her to find three sensational professional *dancers* to take the place of the boy mice."

"What?" Ryder protested. "Days and days of work, and we aren't going to be a part of the audition?!"

"Exactly," Ruby said. "You'll come in at the end, so the teachers won't *notice*!"

"How in the name of cheese can you **replace** Ryder, Craig, and Sebastian with three strangers?" Zoe cried. "The professors will be sure to notice!"

Ruby smirked and took three large masks from a package that had arrived that morning. "With these on, no one will be able to tell them apart!"

The mice were squeakless: Ruby had thought of everything!

Ryder was the first to **react**. "How dare you treat us like this?" he spluttered. "You've gone **too far** this time, Ruby!"

He turned and stormed out of the room, with Craig and Sebastian at his paws.

Let's go . . . .

FRIENDS TOGETHER

The Thea Sisters and their friends scurried back to campus to start planning their new dance. They ran into Ryder, Sebastian, and Craig as they were heading toward the gym.

"What's up, ratlets?" Paulina asked, noticing their dejected expressions.

"We're out of the audition!" Sebastian burst out.

The ratlets told the Thea Sisters' team what had happened.

"So, after STEALING our music," Nicky said incredulously, "Ruby seriously has the nerve to replace you with professional dancers?!"

"I can't believe it," said Craig, shaking his

snout. "All that work for NOTHING! And now we won't even get into the class . . . ."

"Wait a minute!" Violet said. "Ruby can't stop you from auditioning, right?"

"No, I guess not," said Ryder.

"Right! So there's a place for you in our dance," Colette said. She winked at them. "That is, as long as you can carry a beat."

Craig grinned. "You Bet we can!"

Soon members of the two teams were hard at work — together!

1:30 P.M.
Pam shows Craig the hip-hop routine.

2 3:30 P.M.
Practice makes perfect!

3 4:30 P.M.
Colette tries to find the right steps with Sebastian.

4 6:40 P.M.
Paulina and Ryder are perfect partners!

5 8:30 P.M.
Practice continues without a break ... well, maybe a little one!

Zzzz ...
Zzzz ...

7 7:25 A.M.
Elly and Tanja work nonstop on the costumes ... with some surprises!

6 10:50 P.M.
While one rodent takes a ratnap, another gets to work!

8 9:15 A.M.
At last, the dance is ready!

AUDITION DAY!

As the mice prepared their performances, the days seemed to fly by. Before they knew it, it was **AUDITION** time!

The teams assembled in the dance classroom, ready to reveal what they'd been working on. Professor Ratyshnikov and her assistant professors were seated behind a **LONG TABLE** at the front of the room. They were murmuring to one another.

"My throat is completely **dry**, Vi," Pamela whispered. "Do you think I'm coming down with something?"

"No, I don't think so," Violet replied, placing a paw on her friend's forehead. "It's just **nerves**. But you're not alone. Feel my paws — they're shaking!"

Just then, Professor Ratyshnikov cleared her throat, raised an **EYEBROW**, and called the first team. "Ruby Flashyfur and her team may begin, please!"

A murmur went through the other students as Ruby's team took the stage. She and her friends were **magnificent** in their elaborate costumes, and the three masked dancers accompanying them moved in perfect **unison**.

The music began, and everything seemed to unfold perfectly. Ruby, Connie, Zoe, and Alicia danced well, and the professional dancers worked to cover up any mistakes their less-experienced partners made.

When the music stopped, the crowd

APPLAUDED enthusiastically. They were all impressed with the dancers' technique.

"It's time to reveal Ruby's **TRICK**," Pamela whispered.

"Wait a second," Colette said. "Maybe we don't need to. Look!" She'd noticed a strange **expression** flitting across the professors' snouts.

Ruby was beaming. But then Professor Ratyshnikov cast the mouselet a look so glacial, it could've **frozen** an iceberg off Coldcreeps Peak.

"We could comment on the technical aspects of your audition," Professor Ratyshnikov said **severely**. "Or the interpretation. But first I'd like to know if the team leader has something to confess."

Ruby turned **PALE** as a mozzarella ball. Professor Ratyshnikov obviously knew that

some of the dancers were **professionals**!

As the students **WATCHED** in stunned silence, Professor Ratyshnikov slowly stepped toward the three dancers.

"**WELL, WELL, WELL** · · · how nice to see you three again," she said. "I could never forget your *TUMBLING*, Brian! Your paws still don't LINE UP with your shoulders, now do they, Steve? And David! I see you've gotten a **furcut**!"

Professor Ratyshnikov knew the dancers that Ruby's mother had hired!

Ruby tried to *explain*, but Professor Ratyshnikov stopped her. "An imposter like you has no place in my class, Ruby! You have proven that the students at this academy lack sincerity and honesty. I am outraged! **I'M LEAVING — FOR GOOD THIS TIME!**"

A SECOND CHANCE

Professor Ratyshnikov was about to storm out of the room when someone **BLOCKED** her path.

It was the headmaster. He'd decided he couldn't let the past repeat itself.

"Camille, you've already made the MISTAKE of leaving once," he said, calling her by the name he had used back when they were **friends**.

Professor Ratyshnikov was squeakless for a moment. "You've already explained your **point of view**, Octavius, and I agreed to give this academy another chance. But I can see that nothing has changed!"

"I'm not talking about the past," the

headmaster continued, "but about the FUTURE: their future!" He pointed to the students, who were watching breathlessly. "Now it's up to you. You have the chance to change the future. You have the **POWER** to behave differently than our former headmaster!"

Please reconsider, Camille!

"What do you mean?" Professor Ratyshnikov cried in **surprise**.

"If you leave again now, you'll punish not just the rodents who **cheated**, but also the rodents who've worked with dedication

and **honesty**," the headmaster explained.

Professor Plié stepped in.

"Professor Ratyshnikov, perhaps we could give another TEAM the chance to show their **work**?"

"I propose that we judge the Thea Sisters' performance!" suggested Professor Plotfur, winking at the mouselets.

Professor Ratyshnikov relented. "All right! I'll allow them to perform."

The Thea Sisters and their teammates looked at one another. They were more nervous than a pack of mice in a lion's den.

But there was no time for that now. The mouselets and their friends SPRANG into action!

THE WORLD
THROUGH DANCE

Shen's music started to **pulse** through the air. He quickly adjusted the stage lights to frame a backdrop inspired by the seaside. Everything was ready for the performers.

Colette and Sebastian swept onstage. They looked splendid in the COSTUMES Elly and Tanja had created. The two dancers performed an elegant sequence of *classical* ballet steps.

Then the music grew in intensity, and it was Paulina's turn. She and Ryder twirled onstage in a stylish tango.

The audience murmured admiringly when the couple stopped in a dramatic pose, their paws woven together.

Suddenly the music changed tempo again, and the spotlight turned to Pamela and Craig, who **BOUNDED** onstage and tapped out a brisk rhythm with their paws. It was an exhilarating **hip-hop** performance!

Then the melody became softer, almost a murmur, and Violet glided forward. She was wearing a layered dress that looked like the petals of a **flower**. She twirled gracefully with her violin, and the sweet sounds of her instrument filled the room.

A moment later, Shen brightened the lights, and Nicky leaped onstage. She whirled through a series of **NiMBLE** jumps and pirouettes, then executed a perfect flip.

For the finale, the dancers came forward together and performed a *LIVELY* combination of dance moves. It was stunning!

As the music ended, everyone held their breath, waiting for Professor Ratyshnikov's **judgment**. Would the teacher remain at Mouseford to direct the new department? Or would she leave the island forever?

Professor Ratyshnikov remained silent for a moment that seemed to last forever. Then, slowly, a *smile* crept across her snout.

"Congratulations to all of you, and thank you!"

she said admiringly. "Your enthusiasm has brought me back many years . . . back to when I was a Mouseford student, just like you. I am impressed by the **originality** of your performance, and the hard work and dedication you put into it."

There was a moment of stunned silence. The mouselets and their friends all looked at one another. Then . . .

"YIPPEEEEEEE!" Pam cried.

The applause that followed seemed to last forever. The Thea Sisters' team couldn't stop hopping up and down like baby bunnies in a carrot patch. They were absolutely overjoyed!

Hooray!

A SPECIAL GIFT

Professor Ratyshnikov had finally made **peace** with the past.

"My dear Octavius!" she cried, embracing the headmaster like an **old friend**. "I want to thank you and your students for teaching me the importance of second chances."

The headmaster shot Ruby and her friends a *STERN* look. "And that's what we're giving all of you: a **second chance**! We'll overlook your cheating this time, but if you betray our trust again, it will be for the last time!"

Then he turned to Professor Ratyshnikov and pulled a small **BOX** out of his pocket. It was the same one she had refused the day of her arrival. "Please allow me to honor you with this special gift."

"For me?" she asked, surprised.

"It's the Seal of the Lizard," the headmaster explained. "For many years I've waited to place this in the paws of the rodent who most deserves it: the one true **founder** of the Lizard Club!"

The Thea Sisters and their classmates **CLAPPED** long and hard.

Shen disappeared for a moment, and then the air filled once again with the **melody** he'd created for his team's PERFORMANCE. Soon everyone was on their paws, dancing!

Professor Plié started to **twirl** with Colette, while Professor Aria and Professor

Plotfur did a wild jig.

"**LOOK!**" cried Nicky.

The headmaster had invited Professor Ratyshnikov to dance . . . and was now awkwardly trying to follow her graceful steps!

Violet winked at the other Thea Sisters. "See, **SISTERS**? I knew this class was going to be full of great **SURPRISES**!"

THEY WERE MORE THAN FRIENDS. THEY WERE SISTERS!

THE
TheaSisters

Don't miss these exciting
Thea Sisters adventures!

Thea Stilton and the
Dragon's Code

Thea Stilton and the
Mountain of Fire

Thea Stilton and the
Ghost of the Shipwreck

Thea Stilton and the
Secret City

Thea Stilton and the
Mystery in Paris

Thea Stilton and the
Cherry Blossom Adventure

Thea Stilton and the
Star Castaways

Thea Stilton: Big Trouble
in the Big Apple

Thea Stilton and the
Ice Treasure

Thea Stilton and the
Secret of the Old Castle

Thea Stilton and the
Blue Scarab Hunt

Thea Stilton and the
Prince's Emerald

Thea Stilton and the Mystery
on the Orient Express

Thea Stilton and the
Dancing Shadows

Thea Stilton and the
Legend of the Fire Flowers

Thea Stilton and the
Spanish Dance Mission

Thea Stilton and the
Journey to the Lion's Den

Thea Stilton and the
Great Tulip Heist

Thea Stilton and the
Chocolate Sabotage

Thea Stilton and the
Missing Myth

Check out these very special editions featuring me and the Thea Sisters!

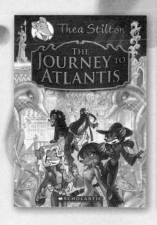

THE JOURNEY
TO ATLANTIS

THE SECRET OF
THE FAIRIES

THE SECRET OF
THE SNOW

Be sure to read all my fabumouse adventures!

#1 Lost Treasure of the Emerald Eye

#2 The Curse of the Cheese Pyramid

#3 Cat and Mouse in a Haunted House

#4 I'm Too Fond of My Fur!

#5 Four Mice Deep in the Jungle

#6 Paws Off, Cheddarface!

#7 Red Pizzas for a Blue Count

#8 Attack of the Bandit Cats

#9 A Fabumouse Vacation for Geronimo

#10 All Because of a Cup of Coffee

#11 It's Halloween, You 'Fraidy Mouse!

#12 Merry Christmas, Geronimo!

#13 The Phantom of the Subway

#14 The Temple of the Ruby of Fire

#15 The Mona Mousa Code

#16 A Cheese-Colored Camper

#17 Watch Your Whiskers, Stilton!

#18 Shipwreck on the Pirate Islands

#19 My Name Is Stilton, Geronimo Stilton

#20 Surf's Up, Geronimo!

#21 The Wild, Wild West

#22 The Secret of Cacklefur Castle

A Christmas Tale

#23 Valentine's Day Disaster

#24 Field Trip to Niagara Falls

#25 The Search for Sunken Treasure

#26 The Mummy with No Name

#27 The Christmas Toy Factory

#28 Wedding Crasher

#29 Down and Out Down Under

#30 The Mouse Island Marathon

#31 The Mysterious Cheese Thief

Christmas Catastrophe

#32 Valley of the Giant Skeletons

#33 Geronimo and the Gold Medal Mystery

#34 Geronimo Stilton, Secret Agent

#35 A Very Merry Christmas

#36 Geronimo's Valentine

#37 The Race Across America

#38 A Fabumouse School Adventure

#39 Singing Sensation

#40 The Karate Mouse

#41 Mighty Mount Kilimanjaro

#42 The Peculiar Pumpkin Thief

#43 I'm Not a Supermouse!

#44 The Giant
Diamond Robbery

#45 Save the White
Whale!

#46 The Haunted
Castle

#47 Run for the Hills,
Geronimo!

#48 The Mystery in
Venice

#49 The Way of
the Samurai

#50 This Hotel Is
Haunted!

#51 The Enormouse
Pearl Heist

#52 Mouse in Space!

#53 Rumble in
the Jungle

#54 Get into Gear,
Stilton!

#55 The Golden
Statue Plot

#56 Flight of the
Red Bandit

The Hunt for the
Golden Book

#57 The Stinky
Cheese Vacation

#58 The Super
Chef Contest

#59 Welcome to
Moldy Manor

*Don't miss
my journey
through time!*

Don't miss any of these Mouseford Academy adventures!

#1 Drama at Mouseford

#2 The Missing Diary

#3 Mouselets in Danger

#4 Dance Challenge

#5 The Secret Invention

#6 A Mouseford Musical

MAP OF WHALE iSLAND

1. Falcon Peak
2. Observatory
3. Mount Landslide
4. Solar Energy Plant
5. Ram Plain
6. Very Windy Point
7. Turtle Beach
8. Beachy Beach
9. Mouseford Academy
10. Kneecap River
11. Mariner's Inn
12. Port
13. Squid House

14. Town Square
15. Butterfly Bay
16. Mussel Point
17. Lighthouse Cliff
18. Pelican Cliff
19. Nightingale Woods
20. Marine Biology Lab
21. Hawk Woods
22. Windy Grotto
23. Seal Grotto
24. Seagulls Bay
25. Seashell Beach

THANKS FOR READING, AND GOOD-BYE UNTIL OUR NEXT ADVENTURE!

Thea Sisters